Ballerina

ENGLISH TRANSLATIONS OF WORKS BY PATRICK MODIANO

From Yale University Press
After the Circus
Ballerina
Family Record
Invisible Ink
Little Jewel
Paris Nocturne
Pedigree: A Memoir
Scene of the Crime
Sleep of Memory
Such Fine Boys
Sundays in August
Suspended Sentences: Three Novellas (Afterimage, Suspended
     Sentences, and Flowers of Ruin)

Also Available
The Black Notebook
Catherine Certitude
Dora Bruder
Honeymoon
In the Café of Lost Youth
Lacombe Lucien
Missing Person
The Occupation Trilogy (The Night Watch, Ring Roads, and
     La Place de l'Etoile)
Out of the Dark
So You Don't Get Lost in the Neighborhood
28 Paradises (with Dominique Zehrfuss)
Villa Triste
Young Once

PATRICK MODIANO

Ballerina

Translated from the French by
Mark Polizzotti

A MARGELLOS
WORLD REPUBLIC OF LETTERS BOOK

Yale UNIVERSITY PRESS | NEW HAVEN & LONDON

The Margellos World Republic of Letters is dedicated to making literary works from around the globe available in English through translation. It brings to the English-speaking world the work of leading poets, novelists, essayists, philosophers, and playwrights from Europe, Latin America, Africa, Asia, and the Middle East to stimulate international discourse and creative exchange.

Yale University Press books may be purchased in quantity for educational, business, or promotional use. For information, please email sales.press@yale.edu (US office) or sales@yaleup.co.uk (UK office).

Set in Source Serif type by Karen Stickler.
Printed in the United States of America.

Library of Congress Control Number: 2024939336
ISBN 978-0-300-27819-4 (paperback : alk. paper)

A catalogue record for this book is available from the British Library.

This paper meets the requirements of ANSI/NISO Z39.48-1992 (Permanence of Paper).

10 9 8 7 6 5 4 3 2 1

Ballerina

Brown? No. More like chestnut, with very dark eyes. She's the only one of whom a photo might still exist. The faces of the others, except for little Pierre, have been obscured by time. Besides, people took far fewer pictures then than they do now.

And yet certain details remain relatively present. I'd have to list them. But it would be hard to put them in chronological order. Time, which has blurred faces, has also erased reference points. All that remains are a few puzzle pieces, forever disconnected.

One evening in November or December, I had come to fetch a child named Pierre in a building in the northwest of Paris, to bring him home. I've forgotten the street name. A massive entrance and one of those elevators with glass-paneled swing doors, so slow and silent that you wondered whether it would come shuddering to a halt between floors. In a large room that must have been the salon, a dozen or so children were gathered. On a coffee table, remains of a birthday feast. The well-heeled woman who had opened the door led me to the back of the room, where Pierre was playing cards with a small blond boy that the woman called Ronnie.

"Your friend has to go home, Ronnie . . . You have to say goodbye now, Ronnie . . . "

And the two of us found ourselves out on the landing.

Outside it was dark. I had taken his hand. Yes, all the children in that apartment were classmates of his from the Dieterlen School, which was in that neighborhood; I sometimes went to pick him up at the end of the afternoon. Ronnie, the little blond boy who was playing cards with him and whose birthday they had celebrated, was his best friend. It would soon be the Christmas holidays, and he was hoping that during them we might take him and Ronnie to the movies.

And so a moment of the past gets encrusted in memory, like a flicker of light reaching you from a star that was thought long dead. Pierre. Birthday feast. Ronnie. Of course he'd go to the movies over Christmas break. I even thought I could take him if his mother was too busy. Walking side by side that evening, we mostly kept silent, but the route was much shorter than the one we sometimes took from school in the afternoon.

We had passed through the gate of the large brick apartment complex at Porte de Champerret. We climbed the cement stairs to the third floor. Hovine opened up, as if he was expecting us. This apartment was quite different from the one we'd just been in. Four rooms off a single hallway. To the left of the entrance, the kitchen with a shower. The windows looked out on the courtyard.

"The ballerina isn't coming home this evening," Hovine said. "She's rehearsing *Train of Roses . . .*"

The ballerina was Pierre's mother. We had given her that nickname. And *Train of Roses*, a ballet she often performed.

Pierre had sat in the leather armchair and was reading a picture book.

"I'll go do the shopping for dinner," Hovine said.

If someone were to show me today two mug shots of his face—front and profile—could I possibly recognize him?

He was of average height. Curly black hair. Light-colored eyes. From what I gathered, he and the ballerina had known each other since childhood.

We were in the first room after the kitchen, the one that served as living room, where the ballerina's friends occasionally got together on the large sofa and the leather armchair where Pierre was now sitting. The next room that opened onto the hallway was the ballerina's bedroom, and Pierre, her son, had the room in the back.

But I don't have a clear memory of the color of the walls. I think they were dark, and today it seems to me that I never saw that apartment in daylight. The light was dim, as if the bulbs in the lamps and the living room chandelier didn't have sufficient wattage.

Hovine put on his usual coat, in herringbone twill. The door slammed shut behind him. The walls must

have been rather thin, since you could always hear footsteps and voices on the stairs.

Pierre was still reading his picture book, open on his
knees. I followed the hallway and entered the ballerina's room. What time would she be back? Late at night,
no doubt. If Hovine had to go out after dinner, I would
be the one to babysit Pierre, and maybe the next morning I'd be taking him to the Dieterlen School. No point in
turning on the lamp in that room: enough light came in
from the windows of the building opposite. I often gazed
at those windows, and after a while I recognized the silhouettes passing behind the glass.

Back in the living room, I saw that Pierre's book had
slid to the floor. He had dozed off, his forehead pressed
against the arm of the chair.

Over the past few days, then, images began coming back to me, in snatches, from a long-distant period of my life. Before this, they had been covered by a layer of ice. Still, at certain moments I had the vague premonition that this wouldn't last. It was fated that sooner or later the ice would melt and those images would float upward, like cadavers rising to the surface of the Seine. And why should this happen now, in a city so changed that it no longer contained any memories for me? A foreign city. It looked like a huge amusement park or the duty-free shops in an airport. A lot of people in the streets, more than I'd ever seen. The passersby walked in groups of a dozen or so, dragging their rolling suitcases, and most of them wore backpacks. Where did these hundreds of thousands of tourists come from? It made you wonder whether they were now the only ones populating the streets of Paris. I was waiting for the red light to cross Boulevard Raspail and saw a man standing on the opposite sidewalk. I immediately recognized Verzini. And I felt a sharp malaise, like finding myself in front of some-one I'd thought long dead.

Maybe it was just a bad dream. Or I was mistaken. Still, I recognized his mass of hair, as thick as ever, no longer black but white as snow, and his face with its heavy features.

I waited for him to cross the boulevard. When he was next to me, at the curb, I turned to him.

"Aren't you Serge Verzini?"

He glanced at me with the same eyes as back then, penetrating and cold.

"No. You're mistaken."

Still that deep voice, which sounded a bit raspy.

He stood there, giving me the once-over.

"Do we really know each other?"

I hesitated in answering. I'd have to give him names, a precise year. But everything got mixed up in my head. I felt like ditching him on the spot, but I finally said:

"Yes, we knew each other once, in the depths of time."

He knit his brow and his eyes grew colder.

"What do you mean by that, 'the depths of time'?"

He was suddenly on the defensive.

"Pardon me . . . I thought you were Serge Verzini."

I had adopted a casual tone, and I even shrugged.

He appeared to think it over for a few seconds. Then:

"Would you like to get a drink, over there?"

And he pointed to the café at the corner of the boule-vard and Rue du Cherche-Midi.

We were sitting at a table facing each other, alone in the room, which surprised me. For some time now, the cafés and restaurants of Paris had been packed. At most of them, there were even lines to get in.

Silence between us. He looked uncomfortable. It was up to me to speak first.

"Do you still run the Magic Box?"

A restaurant where, on Saturdays, they used to host a "dinner theater." Peculiar routines, performed one after the other in quick succession by players who were themselves just as peculiar. But we mainly went there during the week and we kept our own company. The establishment was located in a narrow side street, not far from Porte de Champerret, where the ballerina and Pierre lived. But all of that belonged to such a distant past . . .

He had smiled slightly. And his eyes had softened. I even think he was looking at me now with a certain compassion.

"The Magic Box? No, that doesn't ring any bells. But I did know, in the depths of time, as you say, some-one named Serge Verzini. Maybe you met the two of us together and got us confused."

The waiter brought us grenadines. He took a long swallow and slowly set the glass back on the table.

"I don't remember much about Verzini. Apart from his name."

I studied his face. It looked less brutal than back when I'd known him. His cheeks had grown sallower, his nose thinner, his eyes appeared smaller and sunken more deeply in their sockets, his forehead taller beneath his white hair.

"Forgive me," he said, "but I have no recollection of you."

"Then maybe you remember the girl we used to call the ballerina and her son, little Pierre?"

"No, can't say I do."

I had the feeling he was evading my questions. I wanted to run other names by him and push back on his resistance, but nearly a half-century had gone by and that was plenty of time for him to forget everything. And even to become someone else in a city where you could no longer find your former bearings.

Through the window, I saw the habitual groups of tourists pass by, as they had for the last few months, packs on backs and rolling their suitcases. Most were wearing shorts, T-shirts, and baseball caps. None of them came into the café where we were, as if this place still belonged to another era that preserved it from that crowd. On both sides of the boulevard, they all headed toward Sèvres-Babylone, in tight ranks.

He had laid his hand flat on the table, and on his index finger I saw a signet ring, its stone engraved with the initials SV, exactly like the one Verzini used to wear when I knew him.

I finally said to him, pointing to the ring:

"Still the same initials?"

"You certainly don't miss much."

He shrugged. Then he pulled from his inside jacket pocket a small leather-bound address book and tore out a page. On it, he wrote something with the address book's pencil.

"If you'd like to get together again, here's my address, mobile number, and also my land line."

He handed me the page, on which was written:

Mobile: (06) 580-015-283

Land line: OPEra-81-60

9 Rue Godot-de-Mauroy (9th arr.)

"Best to call on the land line."

Outside, we were jostled by the flood of tourists. They advanced in compact clusters and blocked our path.

"Maybe someday we'll pick up the conversation," he said. "It's all so far in the past. But I'll try my best to remember . . . "

He just had time to wave goodbye before being carried off and getting lost in that fleeing army that cluttered up the boulevard.

Sometimes, in dreams, one rediscovers the light of those years, as it was at certain specific times of day.

The ballerina would arrive at the Gare du Nord at 7:45 in the morning. Then the metro to Place de Clichy. The building housing Studio Wacker was run down. On the ground floor, a dozen or so used pianos, placed haphazardly as if in a warehouse. On the upper floors, a kind of dining hall with a bar and the dance studios. She studied under Boris Kniaseff, a Russian who was considered one of the great teachers . . . A particular smell of old wood, lavender, and sweat. She rubbed elbows with dancers of all types: Opéra headliners and music hall hoofers, Jean-Pierre Bonnefoux, Marpessa Dawn, and others whose names I've forgotten.

When her lessons were in the afternoon, she finished at about 7 p.m. Why is Studio Wacker associated with the months of autumn and the beginning of winter, early in the morning when it was still dark and at the end of the afternoon when night had already fallen?

At those hours, it felt like you were melting into the city. You walked and you were but a mote of dust amid the other dust in the streets. Soon she no longer needed to take the evening train at the Gare du Nord, to go back to a distant suburb. The room she rented on Rue Coustou was right near Studio Wacker. You only had to skirt the façade of the Lycée Jules-Ferry and follow the boulevard up to Place Blanche. Even in early winter, there was a certain softness in the air. And when it was cold, the lights of the boulevard were even brighter and more welcoming. Just before Christmas, they set up fairground stalls on the median strip. And those dance terms that recur in my memory, without my being able to say today precisely what they meant. The diagonal. The variation. The déboulé. The floor barre. I still find myself reciting them in a murmur. Also, learning to "soften the elbows" to give an impression of fragility. Yes, soften the elbows. Dance, Kniaseff used to say, is a discipline that enables you to survive. One evening, he was sitting with her at the bar in Studio Wacker, in the muted light. They were alone, class having ended long before. He told her that this discipline gives real meaning to life and keeps you from drifting. He himself . . . She was amazed that he should confide in her, he who was normally so reserved, observing a kind of military rigidity. Do you know why the Russians have excelled in this discipline better than anyone? Because many of them have had to struggle against their internal chaos, their violence, and the melancholy that comes over them periodically. And he burst out laughing, as she listened to him with mouth agape. "You are my favorite pupil, and you mustn't be afraid of suffering and bleeding into your dance slippers. You understand?" It was the first time he'd really spoken to her. During the lessons, she had so little self-confidence that she never would have imagined him paying any particular attention to her. It's true that she often found herself with dancers who were older than she, more seasoned. And that evening, he had told her she was his "favorite pupil." And he had even added, alluding to one of his former students: "If you keep it up, you'll be as good as Chauviré . . . "

They had parted company at the entrance to the studio building, and she had stood there, immobile, following him with her eyes until he disappeared down Boulevard des Batignolles in his old anorak, his beret pulled down to his eyebrows. Watching him from behind, it seemed to her that Kniaseff was so light his feet barely touched the ground. That's what dance is, he frequently told his students. So much work to give the illusion that you lift effortlessly several feet off the ground . . . She walked beneath the trees of the median, in a state of exhilaration. She repeated to herself the words he'd said to her: "You are my favorite pupil." Climbing up to her room, she hadn't even felt the stairs.

I never really learned how she'd gotten to know Hovine. She had told me he was a childhood friend, from when she lived in Saint-Leu-la-Forêt. I met Hovine for the first time the evening when the three of us went to pick up Pierre at the Gare d'Austerlitz.

Up until then, I hadn't known she had a son. We were almost half an hour early. Pierre was traveling on his own and she was afraid he'd get lost. We sat on a bench in the station waiting room, as near as possible to the track where his train was due to arrive.

When the train entered the station, we posted ourselves at the entrance to the platforms. She searched anxiously in the flow of passengers, not seeing Pierre amid the crush of people. After a while, the crowd thinned out and only a few scattered individuals remained. We walked back up the platform. It was Hovine who spotted Pierre climbing down from one of the last cars, as if he'd been afraid, until then, of getting lost in the swarm.

She seemed intimidated by her son. He, too, was clearly feeling some reserve toward her. They stood facing one another, as if observing each other, before she leaned down and planted a clumsy kiss on his cheek. I wondered how long it had been since she'd seen him last. I never got an answer. Most often, with her, things remained vague. On the lapel of Pierre's coat, I noticed a label on which someone had simply written his first name, as they used to do for children evacuated by train during the war. Hovine carried his valise, a small valise made of tin. There weren't too many people at the taxi stand. She slid in with Hovine and Pierre on the back seat and I sat in front.

Pierre watched the passing landscape through the window. Did he know Paris? If this was his first time, he would surely keep a memory of this ride through town. But would he remember the people who were with him? We arrived at Place de la Concorde, and I turned around to face him. All the bright streetlights were apparently making an impression. She, too, was silent. It must have been a long separation, since she couldn't find anything to say to him.

The taxi stopped in front of the cluster of buildings on Place de la Porte-de-Champerret. She'd moved in only a short time before, and that was why she'd had Pierre come to Paris.

"I hope you like your room."

He didn't answer. He raised his eyes to take in the building façades.

That was the most uncertain period of my life. I was nothing. Day after day, it felt like I was drifting in the streets and that there was no difference between me and those sidewalks, those lights, to the point of becoming invisible. And yet I had the example of someone who practiced a difficult art—"very, very difficult," as Kniaseff repeated in his Russian accent, an accent so light that it sounded British or Viennese. And I do believe that the example the ballerina set, without my fully realizing it, incited me to gradually change my behavior and shed the uncertainty and nothingness that filled me.

Sometime before I met her, I was looking to rent a room, and I remember walking one late afternoon into a real estate agency on Place de la Madeleine, having spotted their business sign. It was 7:30 and the man who opened the door for me said it was too late to see clients.

He nonetheless led me through the deserted rooms to his office. He asked me how much rent I could afford. Three hundred francs. "That's not very much," he said, sucking pensively on the tip of his ballpoint pen. Given his lack of enthusiasm, I was about to leave, when he added: "I might have something for you." And he told me about a man who rented out rooms in the neighborhood. "I'll give you his phone number. You can say I told you to call."

I called this Serge Verzini and he agreed to meet me in front of a building in one of those streets near the Madeleine church. The room was under the eaves and tiny, at the far end of a long corridor dotted with doors, each with a number on a small enamel plate. Mine was number 23. Then he took me to a bar on Rue Godot-de-Mauroy to "sign the contract," a bar with light-colored wood that he owned. I had wondered what he did for a living, when he'd shown me the room. But here, sitting facing each other on leather armchairs, it occurred to me that his black, slicked-back hair, the rather brutal features of his face, and the elegance of his clothes corresponded to the décor of our surroundings.

He explained that he owned every room along the corridor, rooms once inhabited by the building staff. But there hadn't been any staff for years.

"Are you a student?" he asked.

"No. I write song lyrics."

Once upon a time he had managed a cabaret in which singers performed. Today he owned a more modest establishment in the 17th arrondissement, the Magic Box. On Saturday nights, they had a "dinner theater," but on the other evenings, it was frequented by a classical dancer and her circle of friends.

"You should come. You'll probably see some fellow songwriters."

Why was he being so nice to me? Perhaps he had a thing for young people . . . There were no customers there that afternoon. The slow hour? Unless no one patronized the establishment anymore, and he, Serge Verzini, sat there all day, alone in his leather armchair.

"If you have any problems with your room, call me."

He hadn't made me sign a rental agreement. He had simply given me his address, or rather the address of the bar, so that at the start of each month I could send him a check for three hundred francs.

Sometime later, I ran into him at around nine in the evening as I was coming out of the building where my room was, on Rue Chauveau-Lagarde.

"So, everything okay with your room?"

I didn't dare tell him the radiator was broken. And winter was coming.

"Are you free this evening? I'll take you to the Magic Box."

I tried to find an excuse. But without asking, he opened the passenger door of his car and motioned for me to get in. He remained silent during the entire ride, which seemed very long. Finally, he turned onto a narrow street, just before Boulevard Pereire.

"Here we are . . . "

A restaurant dining room poorly lit by diminutive table lamps. A bar at the entrance. A platform in back that might have served as a stage. Stuffed armchairs against the wall, near the bar. He pulled me toward a table in the restaurant where two young people were sitting.

He gestured for me to take a seat and he also sat down, next to me. He seemed to know these two people well.

"A friend who works in songs," he said, introducing me to the girl.

"Oh really? In songs?"

She looked at me with what appeared to be an ironic smile.

"And she is a great dancer, you know," Verzini told me.

Then he got up, leaving me alone with them, and went to join two men sitting in the armchairs near the bar. I have only a disjointed memory of that evening, as if it had unfolded on a staccato rhythm, faster and faster. Who was the man at the table with the ballerina that evening? It could not have been Hovine, whom I met later, or Jean-Pierre Bonnefoux, who studied with her under Kniaseff at Studio Wacker. We exit the restaurant, and the man with her, whose face has been erased forever, leaves us on the sidewalk. I am alone with her. She tells me she needs to walk and that her building isn't far away. I offer to accompany her.

We follow Boulevard Pereire, then Avenue de Villiers. The air is warm, almost like in summer, and yet I seem to recall it was in the month of November. And I'm certain that the trees hadn't yet shed their leaves.

There were many other such strolls. Leaving Studio Wacker, she said she needed to walk. I waited for her class to finish, sitting at the back of the studio so as not to disturb anyone, in the recess of a window overlooking Rue de Douai.

She had introduced me to Kniaseff as a "songwriter," and he had said with a suspicious air: "Why? Are you trying to get her to sing?" Then he had eventually gotten used to my presence. In the evenings, we returned on foot from Studio Wacker to the apartment at Porte de Champerret. Sometimes, Kniaseff left the studio with us and followed the same route along Boulevard des Batignolles. We kept silent. We left him at Carrefour Villiers, and I had the feeling he was going to keep walking aimlessly for quite a while.

"Do you live near here?" I'd asked him.

"Oh, no! A long way . . . a long way from here," he said in a sad voice.

We felt bad about leaving him on his own.

Last night, I tried to draw up a list of the people who formed a small group around her. First, a few dancers from Studio Wacker, whose names I still recall: Jean-Pierre Bonnefoux, Félix Blaska, Marpessa Dawn, Lebercher, Jeannette Lauret, Michel Panaiev, Nicole Jade . . .

We met them in the studio cafeteria and, after class, at the Bastos, on the boulevard near the Gaumont Palace.

Sometimes they came to the apartment at Porte de Champerret. And then there were others who visited the apartment more often. Hovine, of course, but also Youra, whose first name is all I remember. He took photos of the productions and wrote articles about ballet for theater programs and a specialized magazine. He was often in the company of a certain Lionel Roc, a former student at the Châtelet dance academy and an impresario. And a tall, athletic brown-haired fellow, Tiouls, a member of the Winter Circus crew. And Peggy Sage, a former dancer who worked in a beauty parlor. And a few faces and silhouettes to which I couldn't affix a name.

And how did Serge Verzini fit into all of this? One day when I was alone with Hovine, he intimated that he and the ballerina knew Verzini because the latter had been close to little Pierre's father. That had all been a long time ago, in Saint-Leu-la-Forêt. And though he could tell that I wanted to know more, he shrugged and fell silent. So did I. It wasn't in my nature to insist. After all, the ballerina, during our long walks, would surely end up confiding in me.

I had noticed a curious detail about the Magic Box clientele. There was the group around the ballerina, a few of whose names I've just given. And then, when Verzini was present, several individuals formed another "group" around him, which had nothing to do with the ballerina's, and whose members spoke among themselves in low voices, as if they didn't want their conversations to be overheard. The Magic Box seemed to be their rallying point. Men, most of them around Verzini's age and with the same dubious sartorial elegance. Occasionally two or three women in furs. And a rather worrisome kind of life-of-the-party type, who went from table to table, with a loud voice, very hard features, and close-cropped hair. He must have been Verzini's business partner and the organizer of the Saturday "dinner theater." His name has suddenly jumped back into my memory, and I honestly wonder why: Olaf Barrou.

Much later, the hazards of my life brought me other details about Verzini and certain patrons of the Magic Box, and even about little Pierre's father. Perhaps I'll come back to this in due course. For the moment, I'd rather not stray down sideroads, but instead follow a very straight path that might let me see more clearly. You have to tread carefully to outwit disorder and the traps of memory.

And so, I remember a large auditorium in the basement of the Rex cinema where she rehearsed with a few other dancers led by a former member of the Marquis de Cuevas's company. The ballet was called *Train of Roses,* one of her favorites. All her efforts to make herself lighter, all that work to "soften the elbows," as Kniaseff said, and give her arms almost immaterial fluidity and fragility . . . Perhaps she would end up flying away, passing through the walls and ceilings and emerging into the fresh air of the boulevard.

The rehearsals in the basement of the Rex lasted about ten days. And every evening there was the return on foot to Porte de Champerret. The walk took longer than the one from Studio Wacker.

At first, I had a hard time keeping up with her, but eventually I got used to her pace. And little by little the feeling of emptiness, of profound stagnation that took hold of me at certain times of day, melted away. It was if she was pulling me along and helping me rise to the surface.

Another walk in Paris that we took together was even longer than the one from the Rex cinema to Porte de Champerret. For the past thirty years, I've searched in vain for the name of that Turk, a great lover of ballet, who every year threw a party for the French and foreign dancers in a minuscule apartment, and I've never been able to determine whether it was on one of the quays of the Bassin de la Villette or along the Ourcq canal. And to this day, no one has been able to tell me, such that I am now the sole remaining witness.

In two adjacent rooms and by candlelight, as if for a birthday, the guests crowded in, among whom I recognized several faces: Nureyev, Margot Fonteyn, Babilée, Bonnefoux, Yvette Chauviré, Jorge Donn, Béjart, and Sonia Petrovna, a young woman whom Kniaseff told us was French but who had adopted a Russian name to dance at the Paris Opéra. Against the walls were sofas on which they took turns sitting. The host, a small, dark, pudgy man with a mustache and black suit, went from one to the other, silent and with an eternal smile. I was always near a window and I couldn't help looking at the landscape through the glass: that basin or canal bordered by low buildings and warehouses where a barge was moored.

Leaving at around one in the morning, we could still hear the din of conversations upstairs in the apartment. All around us, along the basin or the canal, was silence. The quays were bathed in a white light. It might happen that, in a dream, you cross through a neighborhood of Paris that seems so distant that, on awakening, you have trouble locating it precisely on a map. And you finally understand that this neighborhood belonged to another city—Rome, London, Vienna, Antwerp—and that, for the space of a night, it had become part of Paris, around the Bois de Boulogne or the Parc Montsouris. Or somewhere else.

Alone, I would have gotten lost. But I trusted her. It was she who guided me.

Try as you might to stay out of reach and feel safe, you can't always avoid ghosts.

The first time she'd been in the presence of that ghost, she was still renting the room on Rue Coustou. That morning, the dance class had been held a bit later than usual, at 10 o'clock. She was walking on the median of the boulevard and recognized him when they were still at a certain distance from one another. She was about to move over to the sidewalk running along Rue Jules-Ferry, to avoid him, but she decided instead to keep walking straight. When she arrived near him, she was overcome by a kind of vertigo and she looked him in the eye.

His own eyes were blank and expressionless. She turned and watched him walk away with even steps, as if nothing had happened.

But several days later, in the afternoon, she was walking along the same route to Studio Wacker. He was sitting, alone, at the terrace of the Bastos, just behind the window. She felt the same sense of vertigo.

She stood frozen, staring at him from the sidewalk. Her eyes met his, which were absent, like the first time. Mechanically, he looked away to watch the café entrance or the clock on the wall. Perhaps he was expecting someone. She hadn't seen him in ages, and at the time she'd worn her hair differently. Probably he hadn't recognized her.

She was relieved to enter Studio Wacker, as if she had crossed the border into neutral territory. Here, she was in no danger. She stood for a moment in the shadows of the ground floor, amid the dozen haphazardly placed pianos. Kniaseff was waiting for her at the studio door.

"You're pale as a sheet . . . Is anything wrong?"

Just hearing his voice made her feel reassured. And as she did her habitual exercises, she regained her calm. The person she'd just seen in the café terrace was only a double. Or simply a harmless nobody, judging by his lifeless gaze.

But the third time she ran into him, she lost her composure. It was a few yards from her building. He was standing immobile on the facing sidewalk, in front of the large garage. She kept walking so he wouldn't see her enter her building. She turned onto Rue des Abesses. He didn't follow her. It was after dark. She decided to wait awhile in the nearby church, the one called Saint-Jean-des-Briques.

She was sitting at the back of the nave. Gradually she regained a sense of calm and the same feeling as at Studio Wacker when she did her exercises: the feeling of reclaiming mastery over her body. What did she have to fear? She stood up, left the church, and retraced her steps. She was walking so fast that it felt as if her feet weren't touching the ground. Again she saw him, immobile in front of the garage, like a mummy that had been abandoned, upright, in its sarcophagus. She pushed open the door of her building. She half expected him to catch up to her in the stairway. But no.

She looked out her bedroom window. Down below, still that shadow, that black stain against the white wall of the garage.

The next day, as she was leaving Studio Wacker, he was there on the opposite sidewalk. He came toward her, a crooked smile on his face.

"Do you remember me . . . ?"

Without answering, she tried to move forward, but he blocked her path.

"Saint-Leu-la-Forêt . . . It's been a long time. Do you remember me?"

She had forgotten his name. He no longer had the spectral appearance of the previous days, the lifeless gaze. It was as if he had been roused into motion one final time before vanishing forever. He gripped her by the shoulders to hold her in place, and the viscous contact nearly made her gag. After eight years, how had he learned that she lived in this area? Who had given him her address and the address of Studio Wacker? She broke loose by elbowing him, a sudden, violent movement he hadn't expected, and she left him behind. Now she was walking on the median of the boulevard.

Saint-Leu-la-Forêt . . . It was as if the name belonged to another life. She would ask Hovine what that revenant was called. Perhaps he had spotted her simply by ill chance and been following her through the neighborhood for a long time. Hovine certainly remembered that period in Saint-Leu-la-Forêt. As for her, dance had made her forget all of it.

But she didn't ask Hovine a thing. She ended up convincing herself it was just a dream, the kind that leaves its stench behind the next day, and even the following days, to the point where it blends with your daily life and you can no longer separate dream from reality. She only hoped the dream wouldn't recur. The best thing would be to change her address.

I had noticed several times, as we were leaving Studio Wacker and on the boulevard near the Bastos, that she would glance behind or around her, as if making sure no one was following. I asked why she looked so worried. She answered in a flippant voice that she was afraid of seeing "ghosts from the past." So who were these ghosts? She gave me a half-smile. Perhaps that day she felt like confiding in someone. It all went back to her childhood and adolescence in Saint-Leu-la-Forêt. There, a woman had given her dance lessons when she was a child, until the age of fourteen. And that woman was the one who'd suggested she apply to Studio Wacker in Paris and had written her a letter of recommendation for Boris Kniaseff. That was when she had begun taking the train from Saint-Leu-la-Forêt to the Gare du Nord in the morning, and in the evening from the Gare du Nord back to Saint-Leu-la-Forêt. She had met little Pierre's father in Saint-Leu. He was a friend of Serge Verzini's, who had a house in that small town. They had even lived in that house for a while. And little Pierre's father? She didn't know what had become of him. Anyway, she no longer thought about it. And Verzini didn't know, either. The people who came to his house weren't always very "reputable." Including little Pierre's father. But Verzini was a fairly nice man and he had helped her out when she decided to live in Paris.

She gave out these details in spurts, in no particular order, as if there were gaps in her memory. For instance, she didn't say a word about her parents, or about many other things. I sensed it was pointless to ask. She wouldn't answer. The past seemed so distant to her that all she had left was free-floating debris. Now she told me about the Balanchine ballet *La Sonnambula,* which she'd been rehearsing for the past two weeks for Félix Blaska's company. In short, her former life no longer interested her and she had sloughed it off like dead skin. Thanks to dance. Kniaseff was right to say that dance is a discipline that enables you to survive.

Abruptly, the name of the "ghost" that she'd run into three times came back to her: André Barise. He had a brother who looked so much like him that she wondered whether he wasn't a twin, whose name she had forgotten. Moreover, everyone just called them the "Barise brothers." And those two words, for her, were enshrouded in a swamplike odor.

Their names were especially linked in her mind to the train trips she made, from the age of fourteen, from Saint-Leu-la-Forêt to the Gare du Nord, and in the evening from the Gare du Nord to Saint-Leu. She often happened to take the 7:30 a.m. train with the Barise brothers and, for the return trip, the 7 p.m. train with just André Barise.

Jowly faces, hard little mouths. Their eyes always stared at you with a shifty look. Thick hands and, in contrast, a precious way of speaking, a vocabulary that they labored to make sound distinguished. And each wore an identical signet ring on his little finger.

It was hard to avoid them. If she suddenly changed carriages to get away from them at the stop in Saint-Prix or Enghien, they followed her. Even if she changed trains at Ermont to arrive instead at the Gare Saint-Lazare.

The evening trips back to Saint-Leu-la-Forêt were the worst. André Barise sat next to her. If she changed seats, he did, too. After Ermont, the cars were half-empty and she could no longer avoid him. He stuck to her. He adopted an increasingly precious tone to tell her about his plans. He worked in an office, but soon he was going to be hired to help make a film, as an assistant at Boulogne Studios. She got up again and took refuge near the exit door. He came to join her and flattened her against the door. She struggled, but he pressed harder against her, so heavily that she was suffocating. The few remaining passengers paid no attention. No doubt they thought it was a game, since Barise threw his head back now and then and laughed out loud.

Getting off the train, on the platform at Saint-Leu-la-Forêt, she started running. She soon put distance between them. He huffed and puffed behind her, and finally gave up. She felt lighter as she ran, and that lightness, that feeling of now being out of reach, she owed to her dance lessons.

But in the morning, when she came across the Barise brothers in the waiting area of Saint-Leu-la-Forêt station, she felt like putting an end to it once and for all.

Only the thought that she would soon be in Paris, at Studio Wacker, brought her peace.

In the evening, at the Gare du Nord, she was overcome by despair at the sight of André Barise. She would again have to put up with him until Saint-Leu-la-Forêt, that guy and his swampish odor.

It was one evening, leaving Salle Pleyel, where she was dancing Balanchine's *La Sonnambula*. A woman had come to the performance, a certain Paula Hubersen, whom she'd introduced to me at the party that the Turk threw for the dancers every year in his small apartment on the Bassin de la Villette or the Ourcq canal.

I'm unsure about the spelling of her name. Paula? Pola? I think it was Pola. Much later, I learned she was the daughter of a composer of operettas who'd had to leave Vienna for America before the war. She was around thirty-five and lived in Paris, separated from an American husband. Like the Turk from the Bassin de la Villette or the Ourcq canal, she was fanatical about the dance milieu. She enjoyed a reputation as a kind of patroness, since she donated money to fledgling companies.

Back then, I lived day to day, never wondering about the individuals that chance brought my way. I let myself by carried by the tide. I floated. Last night, at the twilight hour, I was alone and couldn't tear my eyes away from a lit window in a building façade. I imagined someone was waiting for me, there, behind the window, to finally respond to the questions I'm asking myself today about that period of my life, questions that have gone unanswered for so long.

Leaving Salle Pleyel, Pola Hubersen led us to her car. She told the ballerina she'd been very moved by her performance in *La Sonnambula,* a ballet she had seen, some years earlier, with Maria Tallchief in the role. Yes, she found her as moving as Maria Tallchief. We climbed into the car, the ballerina in front and me on the back seat. Pola Hubersen wanted to take us to dinner near her home, in one of those wide avenues that fan out from Place de l'Etoile.

A place you couldn't have spotted in this deserted neighborhood. You entered through an unmarked door, as if it were a speakeasy. In contrast with the darkness outside, the harsh light in the small dining room made you squint. A mahogany bar. Several tables were set beside a thick curtain, which they had no doubt pulled shut to keep the light from filtering out. Given the late hour, we were the only patrons.

Pola Hubersen was apparently a regular, as the man who seemed to be the manager and whom she called by his first name immediately brought her a bottle of whiskey and a glass. And the ballerina didn't seem surprised by this. She must have been familiar with Pola Hubersen's habits for some time.

Why has that evening remained so present in my memory? At first, I'd felt as if I had no points of reference. The place where we were seemed cut off from the world, with its curtains drawn shut against the wide deserted avenue that sloped down toward the Seine. If I had left the ballerina and Pola Hubersen and found myself outside, on the sidewalk, I don't believe that feeling would have dissipated. I would have walked straight ahead, not recognizing the city around me, and sought out the nearest metro station for reassurance; but at that hour, the station gates were locked shut. Who could I ask for directions? The ballerina and Pola Hubersen were talking between themselves and ignoring my presence. Pola Hubersen regularly poured whiskey into her glass with a graceful gesture and drank it in little sips, the alcohol apparently having no effect on her. I labored to follow their conversation, thinking that their words were now my only reference markers: Maria Tallchief . . . Babilée . . . Rosella Hightower . . . Michaël Denard . . . Béjart . . . Maybe you should be in that company . . . You were so good in *Train of Roses* . . .

Pola Hubersen turned to me and asked in a very gentle voice:

"And what about you, are you interested in dance?"

I jumped. Until then, she hadn't paid me much attention.

"Yes, I'm interested."

I tried to find the words. I was so surprised that she should speak to me . . . And I've always had trouble answering questions.

The ballerina came to my aid.

"He's interested because he considers it a discipline. A discipline that enables you to survive, as Kniaseff always says."

Pola Hubersen kept her eyes fixed on me. Apparently, what the ballerina had just said impressed her.

"Do you need discipline?"

She seemed to want to know more.

"Yes, unfortunately."

"Why 'unfortunately'?"

"Because, at the moment, I don't have any."

Her face was serious. She seemed to be taking this thing to heart.

"But surely you'll end up finding a discipline . . . "

"Don't worry about me, it'll happen, it'll happen . . . "

And I forced myself to smile and give a slight shrug, to break the serious turn the conversation was taking.

Outside, we walked down the avenue. She had proposed we "have one last drink" at her place, and the expression made me smile. Neither the ballerina nor I ever had any drinks.

I felt reassured in their company. One or perhaps two in the morning. The locked gates of the metro stations didn't matter, or the deserted avenue and the dark windows of the buildings that made it seem as if no one lived there anymore. Or the silence around us.

We turned onto a narrow side street. She opened the building's entrance door and let us pass in front of her. In the dark, she patted the wall, looking for the light switch. No need to take the elevator, the apartment was only one flight up. A foyer. A fairly spacious salon with windows overlooking the street. A certain untidiness. An African mask on the floor, between two windows. Statuettes of Shiva and Ganesh on the mantelpiece and on a coffee table, in front of a wide sofa layered in cashmere shawls. Paintings stacked against one another as if for a move had left outlines on the walls.

We were seated, the ballerina and I, on the wide sofa. She came to join us with a tray that she set on the coffee table, amid the statuettes. She filled three glasses with a liqueur whose name I couldn't read on the bottle. I took a sip. A very strong liqueur. Pola Hubersen took a large gulp. The ballerina, not a drop. And I suddenly remembered something that she'd told me Kniaseff often said to his students: "Dancers don't need alcohol, because dance is the strongest liquor of all."

I don't know how long we sat there. She had put on a record of Hindu music, whose tones and silences penetrated me with a throbbing sweetness. And the faces on the ballerina and Pola Hubersen suggested that at that moment, they were feeling the same thing.

"It's cold in here, don't you think?" Pola Hubersen asked us.

"It's a bit chilly," said the ballerina.

"They shut off the heat yesterday. We'll be more comfortable in my room."

She walked ahead of us down the hallway. The ballerina had taken my hand, as if to lead me on a path that she already knew.

The bedroom was as large as the salon, but there was only one window behind the red drapes. A small lamp sat at the edge of a bedside table cluttered with books. She lay down next to the bedside table and invited us to follow her example. The ballerina was between Pola Hubersen and me. The bed was narrow. Pola Hubersen turned off the lamp and slid closer to us. All that remained was a shaft of light from the hall, spilling from the half-open door.

The day after the one when the ghost was waiting for her in front of Studio Wacker and when she fended him off with an elbow to the stomach, she telephoned Verzini. Could she see him right away? He told her to come join him at the bar on Rue Godot-de-Mauroy.

He was there, sitting at a table, alone. He hadn't removed his coat and he was wearing snow boots. It had snowed overnight. When she came in, he stood up to light the wall lamps at the bar.

She remained standing, looking embarrassed.

"Have a seat. Would you like some coffee?"

He turned on the percolator and set two cups on the table. He looked at her with a smile.

"To what do I owe this morning visit?"

But she remained silent. He took her hand.

"Is something wrong?"

Finally, she found her resolve. In rushed tones: "Someone's been bothering me. Someone I knew long ago in Saint-Leu . . . André Barise . . . There were two brothers . . . the Barise brothers . . . "

He knitted his brow. She awaited his answer.

"Barise . . . Right, of course . . . The family lived on Rue de l'Ermitage . . . near my house . . . The parents had a small silk shop in Paris. I could even tell you where: Rue Olivier-Métra . . . You see? I still have a good memory . . ."

Well, this André Barise knew her home address and the address of Studio Wacker. Eight years earlier, the two brothers were constantly harassing her in the trains she took to Paris for her dance lessons, and in the evening on her way home. And after all these years, yesterday, in the street, André Barise had tried to block her path and she had elbowed him hard in the stomach to get rid of him.

Verzini appeared lost in thought.

"We'll have to teach that boy a permanent lesson . . ."

Arms folded on the table, he leaned toward her and said in a murmur, as if afraid someone might overhear: "Don't fret. The first thing is for you to change apartments."

That was precisely what she'd wanted to ask him about.

"I have a place that's empty at Porte de Champerret. You can move in there, if you like."

She felt as if a weight had been lifted.

"Just let me know what time your lessons are at Wacker. I'll have someone keep an eye on the area. Do you feel better now?"

He spoke to her as if to a child.

"So, you elbowed him in the gut? Next time I'll be the one to handle it and it's liable to be much more painful. Assuming he makes it out alive."

And he suddenly burst out laughing. He gazed after her as she walked up the street toward the Grands Boulevards. She walked on the patches of snow and black ice, light on her feet—like a dancer, he thought; anyone else would have skidded and fallen heavily. What a strange girl . . . She hadn't changed since she was a child, when he had known her with her father, and much later with the father of little Pierre.

One day, she and her father had been in his house in Saint-Leu-la-Forêt. Looking at the two of them, he'd had the premonition that the man's failings would be transformed, as if by magic, into qualities for the little girl. It would seem the future had proven him right.

She had to wait until six o'clock before Verzini could show her the apartment at Porte de Champerret and give her the keys. She had missed her dance lesson, and whenever she couldn't submit to that discipline under Kniaseff's instruction, it left her feeling strangely empty. According to Kniaseff, the body first had to exhaust itself to reach a state of lightness and of fluidity of movement in the legs and arms. And the word "exhaust," which he pronounced with a Russian accent, had at first been incomprehensible to her. Once, when the two of them were alone together, he had explained what that meant: yes, it was about "loosening the knots" through exercises, and it was painful, but once they were "loosened," you felt a great relief, that of being freed from the laws of gravity, as in dreams when your body floats into the air or in the void.

She walked haphazardly. She was used to doing this, and often for long stretches at a time, even after dance lessons. No doubt about it, Kniaseff was right: the body had to exhaust itself.

But that morning, walking wasn't enough. So she tried to think about something else—about Verzini, who had just done her another favor, as he had for years. Perhaps in memory of little Pierre's father? But they never spoke about him, and Verzini didn't know what had become of him. She had asked him once. "He was reckless," was all Verzini said. She remembered Verzini's house in Saint-Leu-la-Forêt, on Rue de l'Ermitage, where she had lived with little Pierre's father. There was often a woman there, whom they called Mrs. Juan, a woman about the same age as Verzini. She had always been nice and encouraged the ballerina when she'd begun taking dance lessons.

One day, she had overheard a conversation between Verzini and little Pierre's father. They were talking about Mrs. Juan. The woman had had a pretty rough life, Verzini said. Her first husband had been murdered, and then her brother-in-law. Settling scores. So to help Mrs. Juan out, Verzini had bought from her the house in Saint-Leu-la-Forêt, on Rue de l'Ermitage, that had belonged to her first husband. Those were the kinds of details she remembered, more or less.

She had lived with little Pierre's father for several months. He was often absent, and then he disappeared. He hadn't counted for much.

From the moment she began taking dance lessons, the early years of her life had been erased like a bad rough draft. She felt like she was born a second time. Or rather, it was at that moment that she'd truly been born.

It was ten in the morning and it had started snowing again. A light snow, practically raindrops. She was cold and felt little pains throughout her body. She had to "loosen the knots," as Kniaseff would say. And so she decided to go to see Pola Hubersen. She was the only one capable of easing her mind. She lay down on the bed, Pola Hubersen stroked her, and her fingers lingered at the right places, with the precision of an acupuncturist. Their lips brushed, and the contact of those lips on her body was even sweeter than the fingertips. Little by little, the knots loosened, without the pain she normally felt at the start of her dance lessons. She occasionally missed a lesson and found herself on the bed with Pola Hubersen. Then she let herself drift with the current, eyes closed.

She took the metro and transferred twice. The trains took a long time to show up and she had difficulty overcoming her impatience. She knew that at that hour of day, Pola Hubersen would be at home. And besides, she had given her a key to the apartment in case she should come by unannounced.

She got off at the George-V stop and walked down the avenue, her agitation growing. She entered the building at the start of Rue Quentin-Bauchart. Pola Hubersen got up very late and perhaps wasn't awake yet. She crossed the foyer, and when she arrived in the salon, she noticed a man's coat on the wide sofa. Pola Hubersen was evidently with someone in her room, and she didn't want to walk in on them unexpectedly. The apartment gave the impression of being narrow: the foyer, the salon overlooking the street, and the long hall that led to the bedroom. But a small door hidden in the wall, on the opposite side, led to a series of rooms along another hallway, most of which were empty, or furnished only with very low settees. She took that path, opened the last door on the right, and went into the large bathroom adjacent to Pola Hubersen's bedroom. The light was on, the door to the bedroom wide open.

She got undressed and slipped on a bathrobe, one of the ones she always wore after a performance and that she had left there. She entered the bedroom. A man was stretched out on the bed, whom she immediately recognized and with whom she had rehearsed a duet at Studio Wacker, a certain Georges Starass. Dancing with him, she had felt something she'd never felt with any of her other dance partners, as if this contact was more intimate than a simple exercise, so intimate that she'd wanted to prolong it.

Now the two of them were alone in the room, and after a few moments she again had that feeling, just like the other day at Studio Wacker, of dancing with him on the same rhythm, in perfect harmony . . . And soon stronger and stronger cries followed on shorter and shorter intervals. Each time, she felt a lightheadedness that expanded to infinity.

At noon that day, we were supposed to go pick up Pierre at the Dieterlen School. I had asked Hovine to drive me there, since it was snowing. I wanted to save Pierre from the school cafeteria, where he had to eat most days. Was it my experience of boarding schools in the mountains, when it snowed as early as November and we huddled in the covered playground during recess after leaving the dining hall, still hungry? I tried to convince the ballerina to spare Pierre the ordeal of the cafeteria, especially in winter, but she looked at me strangely. Apparently she didn't understand my qualms. And yet, I intuited that her childhood and adolescence had been harder than mine. No doubt she deemed that eating in the cafeteria was no big deal for a child.

On the way, I asked Hovine about the ballerina and Pierre. But he answered evasively, as if he was afraid of betraying a secret and that the ballerina would find out. Didn't she sometimes tell him he was "too talkative"? Talkative? That wasn't the impression he gave me. When

I was with him, there were notably long moments of silence between us.

"So you think we should leave him at the cafeteria?"

"Oh, it's no great hardship."

He smiled at me. He, too, I imagined, had had a difficult childhood and adolescence.

"The main thing is that we look after him," he said. "The ballerina doesn't always have time, what with her rehearsals and ballets."

Then, in a tone that might have been sarcastic or admiring, I couldn't tell which:

"You know, the ballerina is a great artist."

We were early and we waited for Pierre in front of the Dieterlen School. He was the only one to come out, as if he received special treatment. His classmates were in the cafeteria. It suddenly occurred to me that we might be setting him a poor example. Too bad. He knew we were going to a restaurant and he'd be able to choose the dessert he liked best.

After lunch, we took Pierre to a movie theater on Avenue de l'Opéra where they were showing Disney films. Then we went home to the apartment at Porte de Champerret. The ballerina was with a certain Georges Starass, a dancer I'd seen two or three times with her and Pola

Hubersen. Kniaseff greatly admired his gifts, even though Starass managed his career somewhat haphazardly. You sensed that dance wasn't his sole interest in life. He often missed rehearsals, and it wasn't always certain that he'd show up onstage for a premiere. I'd gathered that he was to perform a duet with the ballerina at the Théâtre des Champs-Elysées. And it wasn't the first time they danced together. Kniaseff had paired them on several occasions during the lessons at Studio Wacker.

Pierre had holed up in the back bedroom to play by himself. I'd very much like to know what became of him. I did some research over the following years, but I didn't know his family name, he who had no family. In dreams, I often gaze at a star in the clear sky, and I'm certain that its distant, irregular light is trying to communicate with me, a light in which bathe the ballerina, Pierre, Hovine, the regulars at Studio Wacker, the apartment at Porte de Champerret, my start in life.

"Are you interested in the world of dance?" Georges Starass asked me.

"It's a matter of chance," I specified. "Chance encounters."

Georges Starass and the ballerina talked of their upcoming rehearsals at the Théâtre des Champs-Elysées. Were these for *The Young Man and Death,* which Babilée had once performed? Or simply *Swan Lake?* Or a revival of *Train of Roses?* I don't remember. It will come back to me later. And besides, it no longer matters in the slightest. I wasn't listening to them. I had met a curious publisher the previous week in a café near the church of Saint-Séverin, a certain Maurice Girodias. We'd started talking because he happened to be sitting at the table next to mine. He had been publishing in Paris a series of English-language novels that were banned in the Anglo-Saxon countries, and he had just opened a restaurant and theater in a space right near there, on Rue Saint-Séverin. If I liked, he'd take me to see it. At first, I was taken aback by his friendliness toward me. But I had listened to him with a level of attention that he probably didn't expect from a young person my age.

After visiting the two floors of his restaurant, then the basement, a vaulted cellar that he wanted to turn into a nightclub, he asked if I knew English. I answered in the affirmative, and he proposed that I work on a book, a typescript of about eighty pages, to which some episodes had to be added. I said I accepted. There are so many ways to get your start in literature . . . And when, that afternoon in the apartment at Porte de Champerret, Starass wanted to know "what I did in life" and I noticed the ballerina's unease when she thought I'd have nothing to answer, I declared in a firm voice, "I write books"—which provoked the ballerina's astonishment, and even a frown, as if I'd just told a lie. But I soon left the living room to go join Pierre in the back bedroom. He was working on a puzzle, one of those huge puzzles that I'd bought for him in a toy store on Faubourg

Saint-Honoré. I helped him fit a piece to the others. The window looked out on the courtyard and on the gray, frozen winter afternoon, the kind of harsh winters that used to exist back then.

At the Théâtre des Champs-Elysées, she continued rehearsing *Train of Roses* with Georges Starass. She had never been attached to a partner by so strong and strange a bond, never felt so powerfully that tension in her body, as if heated white-hot by dance. She knew the bond would not last. When the rehearsals and performances were over, life would pull them onto different paths.

One evening, as she was coming out of the metro at George-V to join Starass in Pola Hubersen's apartment, she thought about Madeleine Péraud, a doctor who had treated her at age fifteen, when she was just joining Studio Wacker; about the woman's patient explanations of complicated things that she eventually came to understand, and about the books on mysticism she helped her discover by having her copy out the most striking passages in a school notebook. One word, among so many others the doctor used, came back to mind: incandescence. She had even given her a short book with a chapter titled "Incandescence."

Incandescence, beatitude, rapture, ecstasy: those terms often recurred in the books the doctor had given her, and she remembered the impression they'd made on her when she read them for the first time. She had ended up thinking that you could use the same words in relation to dance.

From the metro station, she followed the avenue up to Pola Hubersen's apartment. The latter was away for two weeks and, whenever the ballerina spent a few hours alone with Starass, it was in that apartment. Night had fallen, a mild night even though it was in the month of December. Soon there would be a final rehearsal of *Train of Roses* with Starass on the stage of the Théâtre des Champs-Elysées. And then, the following evening, the premiere of the ballet, the curtain calls and applause, during which the body remains tense from the effort, then relaxes. And after that, she would likely never see him again.

That evening, as she approached the apartment, she felt an acute sensation rise in her that would grow more intense when they were in the room together. They had rehearsed that morning, and now he was waiting for her in the bedroom. She tried to walk with calm steps and it made her heart beat faster. It was like the feeling that comes over you as you go onstage to join your dance partner. But more violent.

She slowly pushed open the door to the building, and when she was at the foot of the staircase she paused for a moment. To climb the stairs, she forced herself to re-create the somnambulist's step that she had used in Balanchine's ballet. On the landing, she took the key-ring from the pocket of her coat. She couldn't settle her nerves and the keys fell. The hall light went out and she felt around for them in the dark. She had trouble fitting the right key in the lock, owing to the trembling of her hand.

When she walked into the salon, she saw his coat folded over the back of the sofa, just where she had seen it the first time. She walked to the sofa, with the lightest possible step, to avoid making any sound. She sat down, her bust rigid and still, knees pressed together, and remained there in the twilight, thinking of him waiting for her in the bedroom. She hesitated about which hall-way to take to go join him, and that hesitation, the time she voluntarily left suspended, gradually lifted her to the point of incandescence. The usual hall off the foyer, or the longer one that led to the bathroom? She heard herself whisper for her own benefit: "The longer hall . . . "

She stood up and started down the hall, maintaining her light sleepwalker's step, but her heart was beating so hard that she suddenly felt short of breath.

Girodias gave me the typescript, whose title was *The Glass Is Falling.* The novel, or rather the novella, was written by a certain Francis La Mure. It was the meticulous description of a group of English women and men who had been vacationing for a long time in a ski resort in Engadine, and their interrelationships, casual yet marked by a certain sexual license.

I asked him if I really needed to add chapters and whether the author would agree to it. He smiled to himself and told me the author would agree. I immediately got to work without asking any further questions.

I worked in the small room I was renting from Verzini, on Rue Chauveau-Lagarde. Ultimately, I wrote only two short chapters, toward the end of the book, and interspersed some paragraphs of varying lengths into the preceding ones. Counting my small cuts to each page as well as my word changes and deletions of modifiers, I'd say it was really more of a copy edit. Before the novel appeared in Girodias's series, with its green covers, the latter wanted to give me a set of galleys and for us to "celebrate" with a private dinner in his restaurant on Rue Saint-Séverin. He had asked me to meet him there at around eleven at night. The restaurant was deserted. What were we in fact celebrating, the publisher and I? A novel, *The Glass Is Falling,* by Francis La Mure, on which I had worked; but I told myself that no one would ever know about it.

That night, I walked along the quays. Shoved into the pocket of my coat were the proofs of *The Glass Is Falling*, and I wasn't sure yet whether I'd show them to the ballerina. She was rather hardheaded and would tell me, in her sarcastic voice: "Yes, but the book isn't yours, it's by Francis La Mure. And besides, it's in English."

Clearly, I couldn't compete with her art. And while the "great artist," as Hovine said, evidently felt affection for me, I always wondered whether she took me seriously.

Despite those doubts, the act of walking along the quays settled me. I had known them for so long . . . I was familiar with every building entrance, the slightest window or antiques dealer's display, one after another, up to Rue du Bac.

Passing by the Hôtel du Quai Voltaire, I regretted not living there, as that spot had always struck me as a magnetic focal point of Paris, at the border of two banks. You just had to cross the bridge to find yourself on the Right Bank, and when you looked out at night from the window of your room, toward the Louvre and the Tuileries Gardens, you felt the future before you, full of promise. To the left of the hotel entrance, behind the plate glass on the ground floor, I saw the bar still lit and two people at a table in back. For a moment, I felt like going in to join them. Perhaps they were waiting for me. Or maybe I was the one who had arranged to meet them there. After all, I was still in that period of life called the "time of encounters."

I had arrived in front of the Gare d'Orsay, decommissioned long before. A dim light shone inside, and if you leaned toward the padlocked fence, you could make out in the semidarkness the former concourse and a row of wooden ticket windows that must have dated from between the wars, or even from the turn of the century. They were much smaller than modern ticket windows, as if people in those days weren't the same size as today. And yet the empty concourse reminded me of the one at the Gare d'Austerlitz, on the evening when the ballerina, Hovine, and I had gone to meet Pierre's train. Yes, once long ago, there had still been crowds in the concourse of Orsay station, and three people—a woman and two men—had come to meet a child and, like us, they'd stood at the entrance to the platforms and tried to spot him amid the flow of passengers. Then they had walked up the platform and seen him disembark from one of the last cars, with his suitcase. And I ended up persuading myself that it was us: for the same situations, the same steps, the same gestures are repeated throughout time. And they are never lost, but inscribed for eternity on the sidewalks, walls, and train station concourses of this city. The eternal return of the same.

I crossed over Pont de la Concorde, and the prospect of returning to my room caused me some apprehension. At the entrance to my building, I'd have to press the light switch and again see that wan, feeble light in the stairway and especially in the endless corridor, each door with its enamel plate. And I was afraid the light would be the same in the apartment at Porte de Champerret, where the ballerina would surely be out, and where I risked waking Pierre and Hovine. It was as if that light impregnated my life, even in daytime. A light that was never clear.

Still, at the edge of Place de la Concorde, it seemed to me that the streetlamps shone more brilliantly than usual and that I was coming out onto a great clearing or an esplanade by the seaside. A breeze was blowing, coming from the Tuileries, or from the start of the long forested avenue, to the left, leading toward the Champs-Elysées. The square was like an oasis in the dark. I breathed in deeply and recovered my buoyancy and natural insouciance. I no longer felt afraid of confronting the wan light of the stairs and corridor. The more I walked, the less my feet touched the ground, like the dancer in the ballet *Train of Roses*. And with that thought, I started laughing uncontrollably.

Sometimes Pierre and I talked, on Thursdays as we came home from the movies. I tried to understand what his life had been like before his arrival that evening at the Gare d'Austerlitz. But a child's recollections are as fragmentary as the ones remaining from my youth. When I think about those few scraps—the ballerina, Studio Wacker, Pola Hubersen and her apartment, Hovine and his herringbone coat—it's like the memories Pierre kept, of a moment, a place, a few phrases he had overheard. And never, later on, would he be able to reconstruct the entire scene, as he did when he finished his puzzles.

He told me, for instance, that the train that had brought him to Paris that evening came from Biarritz. The ballerina had never wanted to provide this detail, other than by an evasive statement: "It was somewhere in the Basque Country." Questions about Pierre bothered her, and no doubt she blamed herself for having abandoned him. As for him, had he been aware of their separation? Apparently not, for he had forgotten the part of his childhood that preceded Biarritz, when his mother might have been around. Only two images from that period had remained in his memory: a clock on a sloping lawn whose face was composed of flowers, on the border of an avenue where they had set up a funfair. He had gotten into a red bumper car with someone who would forever remain unknown to him. There was a dog somewhere, but he couldn't say where.

Of Biarritz, he remembered "Saint Mary's," his first school, where they gave you a "cross" each week when you'd been a good pupil, and the place where he lived, near the school and the "chateau Gramont." And the very tall waves that frightened him on stormy days, and the words *"Toro de fuego,"* which he had often heard but didn't understand. And also the face of the woman who took care of him, but he had never wondered who she was, exactly. Enough to make you believe that children never ask questions and find nothing out of the ordinary.

I took him to the Bois de Boulogne when it was nice out. The bus, the lakes, the boats, the Chalet des Iles with its miniature golf . . .

Most of the time, during our walks throughout Paris or on bus rides, we didn't speak. The silence between us was a much stronger bond than words. We were like those people who walk side by side, never saying a thing but always taking the long way around.

The other day, in this year 2022, I was walking on Rue Notre-Dame-des-Champs. A car was parked along the sidewalk, almost at the intersection with Rue Vavin, and a man was sitting at the wheel, his window lowered.

"Hey, you . . . Mr. Elegant . . . "

He was leaning out the car door, staring straight at me. A man about my age. His skin was slightly pock-marked. And his hair was still brown. But maybe he dyed it.

I continued on my way. Behind me, I heard again, this time louder:

"So, Mr. Elegant . . . You don't recognize me any-more?"

I don't know what abruptly came over me. I made a sudden about-face and strode back to where he was. I said with surprise in my voice:

"Are you calling *me* 'Mr. Elegant'?"

We had been living through difficult times for the past three years, the worst I'd ever known. And the world around me had changed so quickly that I felt like a stranger in it. I was wearing an old black parka, rumpled tan trousers, and shoes with crepe soles. No, this wasn't a time for playing at being elegant. More like for keeping a low profile.

He looked me over with a smirk.

"Ah, Mr. Elegant . . . You haven't changed a bit . . . Still in touch with the old gang from the club?"

"The club?"

He had mistaken me for someone else, but at my age you end up not being sure of anything anymore. Maybe I'd once worked in a "club," as he put it, and had since forgotten. And maybe sometimes we had a collegial drink together, in the evenings after work.

"As for me, I left the club ten years ago."

I studied him as closely as I could. Truth to tell, he didn't look familiar. But I knew how drastically facial features could change in fifty years. Nose. Lips. Eyes.

"So, you've lost touch with the old gang from the club?"

Now he was speaking not only in a mocking tone, but rather aggressively. And I didn't have the slightest memory of that face with its pockmarked skin.

I stood near him, lost in thought. A man who looked like me, who perhaps even *was* me, had been his colleague, but he was apparently unable to tell me his name and the name of our "club." He was content simply to keep repeating, while staring at me with a hawklike gaze and nodding his head:

"Ah . . . Mr. Elegant . . . Mr. Elegant . . . "

What good was it to insist? I took advantage of a brief lapse of attention on his part, as he was searching for something in his jacket pocket, and walked off quickly toward Rue Vavin. After a second, I heard him shouting in a threatening voice: "Hey, Mr. Elegant . . . Turning your back on your old friends, Mr. Elegant . . . ?" He had stepped out of his car, and for a moment I was afraid he was going to come running after me. But compared with the harsh and incomprehensible world in which we'd been living for some time, the episode was inconsequential.

Elegant. It was a word that was often on the ballerina's lips, whether in reference to her profession or to daily life. An "elegant" dancer, an "elegant" performer, she repeated about certain of her colleagues, and it meant that their movements were especially graceful and light. She said it constantly about her partner Georges Starass, but she seemed to apply that judgment more to the nonchalant way he led his life. And it was enough for her to cross paths with someone in the street or to be in the presence of a newcomer to say, "So elegant . . . " She said it about Pierre, on the rare occasions when she saw him playing in his room or heading off to school.

Once, I teased her gently by asking, "And what about you, are you elegant?" She shot me a sad look: "Oh, no. Not in the slightest."

One afternoon, I had gone with her to Repetto so she could buy some dance slippers and tights, and we'd ended up in a deep, narrow bar on Boulevard des Capucines, the Hole in the Wall, where she sometimes met her dancer friends from the Opéra.

The place looked as if it hadn't changed since the thirties, like a bedroom long walled off that you discover when knocking down a partition in an apartment, with its period furniture, its unmade bed still bearing the imprint of a head on a pillow, and the evening paper lying on the nightstand, its headline announcing the assassination of President Paul Doumer. No doubt that was why the bar was called the Hole in the Wall. From outside, it was very difficult to spot the entrance in the dark wall.

"So," she asked, "have you found a job?"

For the first time, she was asking me a pointed question about "my work." She thought I didn't have any, since I never talked about it. I was always very discreet about anything concerning me. My life had unfolded up till then in a certain solitude that hadn't predisposed me toward confiding in people.

"Yes, I found a job. Working for a publisher. He gave me a book in English to edit."

She frowned.

"A book in English?"

"He's publishing a line of books in English. His house is called Olympia Press."

I had made my voice deeper when saying "Olympia Press." I wanted to convince her that this was a legitimate business.

"I take out sentences and adjectives. And I insert a few paragraphs. I also have to write two additional chapters. It's a kind of exercise, a little like when you do exercises at the barre."

The comparison didn't seem to persuade her. And I felt a little ashamed at having compared my copy editing to the exercises I'd often seen her do at Studio Wacker. And yet ever since that time, I've been convinced that literature was also a difficult exercise, like dance, but in a different form.

"So you make your edits in English, is that right?"

"No, in French. It's more natural for me. Olympia Press will translate them into English afterward."

"Will you show me this book?"

I wasn't entirely certain it would ever appear. And she, too, seemed dubious about the outcome of the project. No point in describing what an odd duck the publisher, Maurice Girodias, was. And especially the kinds of books that made up his series with their dark green covers.

Besides, we never spoke much about literature. In her room, a hundred or so books were lined up on two very low shelves near her bed. They were split between detective novels and works devoted to the experiences of women mystics: Saint Teresa of Avila, Claudine Moine, Sister Marie des Vallées, Louise du Néant, Hadewijch of Antwerp . . . They bore on the half-title page a name written in pencil: Madeleine Péraud.

That day, from the Hole in the Wall, she offered to walk me back to my room on Rue Chauveau-Lagarde. The light in the stairs and in the long corridor seemed less muted than usual, thanks to her presence. It was the first time she'd visited and she looked with some surprise at the aged wallpaper, the window overlooking the rear court, the sink, the table.

"Verzini could have found you something nicer."

But when it came to her, she wasn't very demanding. She remembered, she told me, asking Kniaseff at around age fourteen if there wasn't a little room at Studio Wacker where she could stay; even a sleeping bag on the wooden floor of the dance studio would have sufficed. Kniaseff had looked astonished. "What about your parents? What do they think of this?" To that question, she had remained silent. Her parents? How to explain to him? It was better not to go into detail.

I pointed out the table where I pursued, as I said to her, "my literary endeavors."

She had sat on the edge of the bed, really more of a cot.

"You should come live at Porte de Champerret."

Sometimes I spent the night in her room. But she often came home very late. She went out with "colleagues," as she said, or went to see their shows. Or she had dinner at Pola Hubersen's. When Hovine left the apartment and Pierre had fallen asleep, I experienced a kind of anxiety, as if she was never going to return. And so, to regain my peace of mind, I read the books lined up on the two shelves. Not the detective novels, all of which I knew, or a science-fiction novel that I'd been surprised to find in her library, *The Dreaming Jewels,* but rather the volumes about the women mystics.

Certain passages were underlined in pencil. By Doctor Péraud? Or by the ballerina herself? I had discovered a school notebook with the ballerina's name on the cover. In it, someone had copied out most of the passages underlined in the books, in an adolescent handwriting that could only have been hers. And on one of the pages was glued a reproduction of a painting depicting the Virgin unknotting a tangled ribbon, whose title was *Mary, Undoer of Knots.* She had found several reproductions on postcards that were stashed in the drawer of her nightstand, and she had given me one with an inscription, explaining simply that it brought good luck.

Had she had a mystical experience at the behest of Dr. Péraud, who had been "a great support for her"? She'd given me no further details about that woman, and I had quickly understood that she would not answer my questions and that she practiced the art of not speaking just as much as that of dancing—those two arts having, in my opinion, certain points in common. I myself had never mentioned to her the school notebook that I'd discovered in her library. I read it in her room while waiting for her to come home around midnight, or sometimes even at two in the morning. More than any long conversation between us, which in any case I knew we'd never have, I felt that those pages allowed me to know her and understand her better. And this, thanks to the passages she had underlined and to certain titles: "The Interior Castle," "The Seventh Houses," "The Letters of Louise du Néant," "The Loner of the Rocks" . . . One day she had taken me to the church of Saint-Ferdinand des Ternes, near the apartment at Porte de Champerret, to light candles, and had confessed that at a certain time in her life, when leaving Studio Wacker, she often sought refuge in the church of Saint-Jean-des-Briques, in Montmartre. But she had said it in a casual voice, as if about a detail that had randomly occurred to her and was of no consequence.

I ended up believing in a connection between those mystical readings and the dance exercises I saw her repeat endlessly at Studio Wacker, all those painful movements to make the body gradually emerge from its gangue and finally reach that realm of beatitude and ecstasy described in the books that Dr. Péraud had lent her. I would have liked to know what the doctor thought of the ballerina. But suddenly I heard the sound of her key in the lock and her steps in the hallway, and that was enough to dispel my grim thoughts.

Someone woke me by knocking loudly on the door to my room.

"It's Verzini."

I went to open it.

"Forgive me for dropping in unannounced. I wanted to talk to you."

He was standing in the center of the room, looking ill at ease. I motioned toward the chair at the little table on which the galley proofs of *The Glass Is Falling* were scattered about. He took a seat.

"Is this your work table?"

"Yes."

I had sat down on the edge of the bed. I too felt ill at ease.

"She told me you don't find this room very comfortable."

"No, no, it's perfectly fine."

"I think she's right. It's my fault. When you came to see me, I had nothing else available."

He sat hunched in his chair. He hadn't removed his coat. The light was cold and gray, and I lit the bedside lamp. A true winter morning, as still existed back then.

"I told her I'd find you something better. As soon as possible."

"Please don't go to any trouble."

He turned toward me. We were facing one another. He leaned his elbows on the little table, his chin in his palm.

"She seems to like you a lot."

He gazed at me in silence, smiling pensively.

"And I've known her for so long that I can't refuse her anything."

I was surprised that this man, with his massive bulk in his coat, would utter those words: "She seems to like you a lot." I would never have imagined such a statement coming from him, who struck me as so abrupt. And her? I had no idea what she really thought of me and I had quickly noticed that confidences were not her strong suit. But I've always distrusted big talkers. And I liked her silence.

"I often stay at the apartment at Porte de Champerret," I told him. "That way I can take care of Pierre."

I couldn't resist asking, "Have you known her long?"

After all, he was the one who had brought it up, so I wasn't being indiscreet.

"Oh yes, very long. She's the daughter of a friend of mine. And little Pierre's father was also a friend of mine.

But younger than me . . . He had to leave France eight years ago."

He looked me in the eye, as if he was about to admit something but was still hesitating.

"How can I explain? We belonged to a somewhat particular milieu."

There was no need for further details, I'd gotten the picture. My father, too, and his friends . . . Despite a certain exterior elegance, a certain friendliness and even kindness that they often manifested in daily life, I wouldn't have been surprised if in some police station they had shown me their mug shots, front and profile. And other photos in which they were seated, wrists in handcuffs.

"She got out of there as best she could," Verzini added. "Thanks to dancing. She acquired a discipline. And I've always tried to help her to the best of my abilities."

He had turned back toward the little table. One by one he picked up the proof sheets of *The Glass Is Falling,* spread out in disarray, and started putting them in order.

"It's a little like you. I imagine you work at this table on all these papers because you too need a discipline."

I was amazed at his insight. It was as if he had seen right through me.

I said, "I'm following the ballerina's example."

He had finished reordering the pages and set the stack delicately in the middle of the small table.

"And what about you?" I asked. "How did things go for you?"

He remained silent for a moment, then said: "Well, I too, at a certain moment, had to put some order in my life."

I was amazed that he used the same words as Kniaseff when he announced the start of class at Studio Wacker.

He stood up. He patted the radiator.

"It's true there isn't much heat in here. You could have told me, you know."

Before leaving the room, he turned to me: "I'll see you very soon. And good luck."

I heard his steps grow fainter, the heavy steps of a night watchman. I had the impression that he was pausing momentarily in front of each door down that long, long hallway.

Walking out of the building, holding her Repetto bag, she thought to herself that the room was way too small for him, especially if he was to pursue his "literary endeavors." Verzini really could have found him something better.

On a whim, she walked to Rue Godot-de-Mauroy. But it was already early afternoon and the bar was closed.

Then she felt a bit disoriented in this neighborhood she hadn't visited in a long while. She felt like turning back and joining him in his room again. But if he'd gone out, she was afraid she might experience the feeling of vacuity that sometimes overcame her when she was alone in the street.

She walked toward the Grands Boulevards. To pluck up her courage and fight off the emptiness, she repeated under her breath, mechanically, a prayer that Dr. Péraud had taught her and that had come back to mind, like a childhood memory: "Most Holy Mary, you who undo the knots that suffocate your children, extend your merciful hands to me." She said it very fast, with no breaks between the words, and it became a refrain that calmed her. And suddenly she understood the reason for her malaise: one early afternoon, eight years before, she had followed the same path, in the same neighborhood between the Madeleine church, Verzini's bar, and the Gare Saint-Lazare, and today she was walking precisely in her own footsteps. She remembered Verzini, that day, alone in his empty bar, face careworn. He had told her that little Pierre's father was waiting for her, right nearby, in the church of Saint-Louis d'Antin.

She knew that church well, as she had been living near it for several months with Pierre's father, on Rue du Havre, in an office building, the entrance to which gave little clue that an apartment was located on the top floor, an apartment that looked clandestine. The church was lost in the midst of the agitation that reigned all day long around the huge department stores, the Gare Saint-Lazare, and the Lycée Condorcet. Swarms of cars and pedestrians.

When she entered the church, he was sitting in one of the last pews, on the left side of the bay. It was early afternoon and the church was empty. She sat next to him, and he told her in a murmur that he had to leave Paris as soon as possible and that she should never go back to their apartment on Rue du Havre. He handed her a leather valise without a word of explanation. He'd write to her. It would be wise for her to leave the church now, before him. She hadn't even told him she was expecting a child.

She found herself alone in the street once more, but this time with a feeling of relief such as she had never known. She was certain she would never see him again and that a new life was starting for her, then and there. Sometime later, overhearing in a conversation the phrases "youthful indiscretion" and "bad company," she thought that she, too, had committed a "youthful indiscretion" after mixing with "bad company." But she had already practically forgotten that man and their last meeting in the church of Saint-Louis d'Antin. What exactly, she wondered, was a youthful indiscretion? Most of the time, practically nothing. At her age, everything scarred over very fast, and soon there was no longer even a trace of scar tissue. No more hostile witnesses. No more traces of anything. Innocence, once more.

She walked, valise in hand, as if she was about to go on a trip. She didn't even need to go on a trip. An hour from then, she'd be at Studio Wacker and starting her exercises under the guidance of Boris Kniaseff, and that was worth more than all the voyages in the world.

But what was in the valise? It wasn't very heavy. Walking up Rue d'Amsterdam, she looked in vain for a bench, an alleyway, a small park, where she could open it without being seen. She couldn't do it right there in the street. She walked into the studio building and snaked among the old pianos to the rear of the ground floor, where the light was weak. She set the valise on a stool. A small key was in the lock. She opened it. Several wads of banknotes squeezed into fat rubber bands. She shut the valise and buried the key in the pocket of her coat.

She was not late for Kniaseff's lesson. But when entering the studio, she felt ashamed at carrying the valise and looked for a place to stash it. She left it in one of the window recesses, without attracting the notice of Kniaseff or the other students. After all, they couldn't have imagined what it contained, and there, at the back of the room, it was no more than an ordinary object.

Kniaseff was about to start his lesson. That afternoon, in his loud voice, exaggerating his Russian accent, he pronounced the ritual sentence, like a signal that marked the end of recess: "And now, Ladies and Gentlemen, let us put some order into all this."

She threw a glance at the valise sitting on the floor, at the back of the studio. Yes, he's right, she thought. From now on, I really have to put some order into all this.

I crossed Boulevard Raspail at the same place where I'd thought I'd seen Verzini, the week before, in this Paris that I no longer recognized. Many fewer people on the boulevard, but still some battalions of tourists, strange tourists come from who knows where, speaking who knows what language if you listened in. They dragged behind them their eternal rolling suitcases and wore the same baseball caps, the same shorts, the same T-shirts. And the same backpacks. What were they walking toward? Toward an army corps billeted in a specific part of Paris? I admit that none of it mattered to me and that I was in a hurry to reach the deserted café where Verzini and I had stopped off, that café that still seemed protected from the harshness of the present moment.

The day after our encounter, I had dialed the two numbers Verzini had given me, the one for his mobile and the one for his "land line," as he said, but neither of them picked up. No point in trying again: I knew very well they would never answer. Was I entirely certain I'd met that ghost? Or was it a dream I'd had the night before meeting him, which I'd let persist into the next day so as to avoid the present?

What had become of the ballerina and Pierre, and the others I'd gotten to know in that same period? That was a question I'd often asked myself for nearly fifty years and that so far had remained unanswered. And suddenly, on that January 8, 2023, it seemed to me that this no longer mattered. Neither the ballerina nor Pierre belonged to the past, but to an eternal present.

I used to believe that the memory of them came to me the way light reaches you from a star that died a thousand years ago, as the poet said. But no. There was no past, no dead star, nor any lightyears that forever separate you from one another, but only this eternal present.

I've kept precise images of a Christmas night when the ballerina had taken us, Pierre and me, to midnight Mass at the church of Saint-Ferdinand des Ternes. She said it was our parish. We leave the church and start for home. The ballerina holds Pierre by the hand. It's the first time I've seen them like that, and I think about Pierre's arrival at the Gare d'Austerlitz, and about their awkwardness with one another on the platform. Then, suddenly, she starts doing a pas de deux with him on the wide sidewalk of Boulevard Pereire. Then another dance step whose name I've forgotten. Then another. And Pierre watches her, laughing. For my part, I imitate Kniaseff's voice as I've heard it so many times at Studio Wacker. "And now, Ladies and Gentlemen, let us put some order into all this." I keep giving orders to the ballerina in Kniaseff's exaggerated accent: "Sorften the elbows . . . Sorften the elbows . . . Grrand jeté . . . Penché . . . Déboulé . . . Battement tendu . . . "

Pierre laughs harder and harder. And the three of us resume our walk in the night, all the way to the depths of time.

PATRICK MODIANO, winner of the 2014 Nobel Prize in Literature, was born in Boulogne-Billancourt, France, in 1945, and published his first novel, *La Place de l'Etoile,* in 1968. In 1978 he was awarded the Prix Goncourt for *Rue des Boutiques Obscures* (published in English as *Missing Person*), and in 1996 he received the Grand Prix National des Lettres for his body of work. Modiano's other writings in English translation include *Suspended Sentences, Pedigree: A Memoir, Scene of the Crime, After the Circus, Invisible Ink, Paris Nocturne, Little Jewel, Sundays in August, Such Fine Boys, Sleep of Memory,* and *Family Record* (all published by Yale University Press), as well as the memoir *Dora Bruder,* the screenplay *Lacombe Lucien,* and the novels *So You Don't Get Lost in the Neighborhood, Young Once, In the Café of Lost Youth,* and *The Black Notebook.*

MARK POLIZZOTTI has translated more than sixty books from the French, including works by Gustave Flaubert, Arthur Rimbaud, Scholastique Mukasonga, Patrick Modiano, Marguerite Duras, and André Breton. His translations have won the English PEN Award and been shortlisted for the National Book Award, the International Booker Prize, the NBCC/Gregg Barrios Prize, and the French-American Foundation Translation Prize. Polizzotti is a member of the American Academy of Arts & Sciences, a Chevalier of the Ordre des Arts et des Lettres, and the recipient of an American Academy of Arts and Letters Award for Literature. He is the author of twelve books, including *Revolution of the Mind: The Life of André Breton, Highway 61 Revisited, Sympathy for the Traitor: A Translation Manifesto,* and *Why Surrealism Matters.* His essays and reviews have appeared in the *New York Times,* the *New Republic,* the *Wall Street Journal, Apollo, ARTnews,* the *Nation, Parnassus, Bookforum,* and elsewhere.